GASTON
Goes to Mardi Gras

GASTON
Goes to Mardi Gras

Written and Illustrated by JAMES RICE

The Illustrator of
CAJUN NIGHT BEFORE CHRISTMAS

PELICAN PUBLISHING COMPANY

GRETNA 1987

First printing, November 1977
Second printing, October 1983
Third printing, December 1987

Library of Congress Cataloging in Publication Data

Rice, James, 1934-
    Gaston goes to Mardi Gras.

    SUMMARY: Gaston the alligator is invited to Mardi
Gras in New Orleans.
    [1. Alligators—Fiction. 2. Mardi Gras—Fiction.
3. New Orleans—Fiction] I. Title.
PZ7.R3634Gas   [E]   77-13302
ISBN 0-88289-158-8

Manufactured in the United States of America

Published by Pelican Publishing Company, Inc.
1101 Monroe Street, Gretna, Louisiana 70053

Designed by Gerald Bower

Gaston loved to swim in the dark, shady waters deep in the swampland of Louisiana. One day he swam near the edge of the swamp where the trees were not so leafy, and bright sunlight streamed through. On a narrow dirt road near the swamp Gaston met a young boy riding a pony.

"You must be Gaston the alligator," the boy greeted him. "I have a message for you from your cousin Alphonse, who lives in New Orleans."

"How about that!" Gaston barked with delight. "Will you read me the message? I forgot my glasses."

"The message is an invitation to Mardi Gras in New Orleans." "Oh? What is Mardi Gras?"

"You have to see it to understand what Mardi Gras is. Come with me. I'll take you to New Orleans where you can meet Alphonse. He'll show you Mardi Gras and tell you all about Carnival."

Quickly becoming friends, the two started toward New Orleans. On the way they met several men on horseback wearing strange costumes.

Gaston and the boy decided to follow the horsemen, who traveled from house to house through the Acadian countryside. The men sang songs and danced and clowned to entertain people on the porches of simple farmhouses. At each house the people presented the men with gifts of chickens and vegetables and also something to quench their thirst.

At the end of the day the chickens and vegetables were mixed into huge pots to make gumbo for the happy crowd that had gathered.

After the gumbo feast, a *fais do do* started and continued until dawn. Everyone sang and danced and made merry.

"What kind of celebration is this?" Gaston asked his new friend.

"This is a Courrir du Mardi Gras, or Mardi Gras as it is celebrated in the country," the boy replied. "It is much different in the city, as you will see."

They journeyed many miles across the swamp to the big muddy Mississippi River, which flows by New Orleans, and Gaston bade his friend goodbye.

Gaston then glided into the water, swam across the great river, and made his way to City Park Lagoon, where he met Alphonse.

The cousins greeted each other happily, and Gaston asked, "What is this Mardi Gras thing you have invited me to?"

"Mardi Gras and Carnival are too much to tell about," Alphonse answered. "I will have to show you. I will start by taking you to a 'den' where the great floats are built for many parades, and I will tell you about Mardi Gras as we look. I have a job guarding the den, because no outsiders are allowed inside the building to watch the floats being made."

They walked to a large building where many people were hard at work. Some worked with hammers and saws, while others molded shapes with paper and paste over wire frames. Still others worked with bright-colored cloth. They were making costumes and draping wooden frames. Everyone worked hard to finish the floats.

"Organizations that present parades with floats or hold balls are called krewes," Alphonse explained to Gaston. "Some krewes sponsor a ball only, and some sponsor both balls and parades."

CARNIVAL and MARDI GRAS

KREWES, TABLEAUX, MARCHING CLUBS and Assorted Groups

Les Pierrettes — BEFORE 12th NIGHT

Twelfth Night Revelers — JAN 6

Carrollton — 2ND SUNDAY BEFORE MARDI GRAS

Atlanteans — ONE WEEK BEFORE MARDI GRAS

Knights of Babylon — WEDNESDAY BEFORE MARDI GRAS

Momus — THURSDAY BEFORE MARDI GRAS

Hermes — FRIDAY BEFORE MARDI GRAS

Mystic Club — SATURDAY BEFORE MARDI GRAS

Mardi Gras, or Fat Tuesday, was the last day of the Carnival season. Carnival had begun on January 6, Twelfth Night of the Christmas season, and the excitement would grow until it ended the night before Lent, with the great Rex and Comus balls.

During the two weeks before Mardi Gras, gorgeous pageants paraded down the streets of

New Orleans and its suburbs every day. Bands played and crowds lining the sidewalks watched. As the days passed, there were more and more parades, the music grew louder, and the crowds became larger.

Nightly, beautiful balls were held throughout the city. On Saturday night came Endymion, the newest of the great parades. The Krewe of Mid-City paraded the Sunday before Fat Tuesday. Its many marching bands came from all over Dixie and competed for an award given to "The Best Band in Dixie."

On Sunday night the Krewe of Bacchus, with a Hollywood celebrity reigning as the god of wine, staged its parade. The Bacchus ball is for visitors to the city, as well as New Orleanians.

The Krewe of Proteus, god of the sea, held its beautiful parade on Monday night, the last parade before Mardi Gras day.

Gaston was thrilled by everything that Cousin Alphonse had showed him.

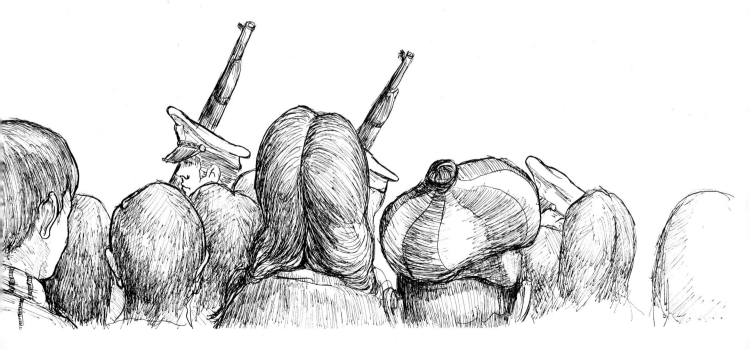

Finally, Mardi Gras dawned, and Gaston and Alphonse hurried toward town to watch the many parades.

On the way they saw crowds forming on the streets, and in a moment they knew why. Zulu was coming!

Soon, the black krewe of Zulu rolled by. Its members were decked out in African costumes and gave out coconuts as they rode by.

"They used to throw the coconuts in the old days," Alphonse told his cousin, "but they decided it was too dangerous."

Jazz bands played Dixieland music, and Gaston joined in the fun, dancing happily along behind them. He even climbed aboard one float and rode for a while (although this is not allowed for mere human spectators).

"So this is what Mardi Gras is all about," Gaston exclaimed. "This is great fun."

"There is a lot more to come," Alphonse assured him.

The other parades began to pass, one by one. Revelers on the floats threw handfuls of sparkling beads and doubloons to the enthusiastic crowd.

Many of the children—and adults, too—
waved their hands above their heads and pleaded,
"Throw me something, Mister."

After a while the two alligators decided to walk on to Canal Street.

As they made their way through the crowds, Gaston spied colorful flags flying at some of the homes they passed. The flags were all alike— green, purple, and gold, with a crown in the center.

"Those are flags of former kings of Mardi Gras," Alphonse told his cousin. "That is the crown of Rex in the center of the flags."

The streets were filled with thousands of revelers wearing all kinds of strange and colorful costumes and masks.

The funniest group Gaston saw that day was the Jefferson City Buzzards. The oldest marching group, it has paraded on Mardi Gras every year since 1890. They marched and pranced and clowned wildly in their curious costumes. A jazz band led the way.

The Boeuf Gras, or Fat Beef, the ancient symbol of Mardi Gras, passed by.

"A Boeuf Gras float has been in every Rex parade since 1959," Alphonse explained. "Historians say its origin dates far back into history."

Rex's parade was the biggest of all, with the Texas A&M University Marching Band leading the way as an honor guard. The bearded Rex wore a shimmering, jeweled costume, and on his head rested a golden crown. He rode on a lavish golden float at the head of the procession.

The krewe stopped at Gallier Hall, where Rex drank a toast to the mayor of New Orleans, and again at the Boston Club, where he toasted his queen, a beautiful young New Orleans lady.

Behind Rex came the truck parades, the Krewe of Orleanians and the Krewe of Crescent City, each composed of more than a hundred decorated truck floats. A young king, from a local orphanage, reigned over the festivities. These authorized followers of Rex always include several thousand costumed participants.

Gaston leaped upon one float as it passed by, flopped his tail, and gleefully waved to the crowd.

The Comus parade was the last procession of Carnival. It proceeded down St. Charles Avenue on Mardi Gras night. It was made up of many beautiful floats and was lighted by flares.

On the lead float King Comus held aloft his golden goblet.

After the Comus parade, Alphonse and Gaston made their way to the Municipal Auditorium where Rex and Comus ruled over separate but lavish balls. The bands played the Carnival theme, "If Ever I Cease to Love," at the Rex ball. Comus, his queen, and their court promenaded before their guests.

Just before midnight, Rex and his court walked over to the Comus ball to pay the traditional visit to Comus, the oldest krewe. At the stroke of midnight it was all over. Another Carnival had ended.

Next morning all was quiet. No one paraded in the streets. Church bells pealed throughout the city.

"Today is Ash Wednesday," said Alphonse, "the first day of Lent." And the priests marked the foreheads of their people with ashes.

"Cousin Alphonse," said Gaston, "now I understand the meaning of Mardi Gras and the spirit of Carnival."

In the countryside, Mardi Gras was a day spent traveling along the parish roads from house to house to celebrate with friends and neighbors.

In New Orleans, it meant working many long days to build beautiful floats and costumes.

It was many parades with floats and people marching in the streets.

It was crowds of people coming from throughout the land, wearing costumes and masks, and joining in the festivities.

It was pretend royalty, with elaborate parades, ceremonies, fancy-dress balls, and much merrymaking.

It was the joyous season before the solitude of Lent.

MOST OF ALL, MARDI GRAS WAS HAV-
ING FUN!